Wolfgran

LIFT OFF!

discover new worlds

Collect O'Brien Red Flag Books

Finbar O'Connor

Finbar O'Connor is a graduate of Trinity College and
King's Inns, and works as a librarian in Dublin. He has
previously published songs, stories and poetry for
children. Wolfgran is his first book. He lives in
Drumcondra with his wife and two daughters.

WOLFGRAN

FINBAR O'CONNOR

Illustrated by Martin Fagan

THE O'BRIEN PRESS
DUBLIN

First published 2001 by The O'Brien Press Ltd.,
20 Victoria Road, Dublin 6, Ireland.
Tel: +353 1 4923333; Fax: +353 1 4922777
E-mail books@obrien.ie
Website www.obrien.ie

ISBN 0-86278-730-0

British Library Cataloguing-in-Publication Data
O'Connor, Finbar
Wolfgran. - (Red flag ; 8)
1.Children's stories
I.Title II.Fagan, Martin
823.9'14[J]
1 2 3 4 5 6 7 8 9 10
01 02 03 04 05 06 07 08 09 10

The O'Brien Press receives
assistance from

the arts
council
an chomhairle
ealaíon
50+

Illustrations: Martin Fagan
Typesetting and layout: The O'Brien Press Ltd.
Colour separations: C&A Print Services
Printing: Cox & Wyman Ltd.

To Margaret, Esmé and Freya

CONTENTS

Chapter One

A Cunning Plan

After her narrow escape from the wolf, Little Red Riding Hood's granny decided that the forest was far too dangerous a place for an old lady to live in alone. So she sold her cottage to the Three Little Pigs (who believed her when she told them it was wolf-proof) and moved into an old people's home in the nearby city.

The Happy-ever-after Home for Retired Fairy-tale Characters was surrounded by a high wall, covered in signs which said 'No Wolves Allowed' and 'Thank You for not Eating the Residents', so Granny was sure she would be safe there.

The wolf started to get lonely, and a little bored, when Granny left the forest. He tried visiting the Three Little Pigs, but they locked the doors, barred the windows and started going on about the hair on their chinny-chin-chins. The wolf just couldn't be bothered with all that huffing and puffing nonsense.

Then, one day, the wolf thought of a cunning plan. If a wolf couldn't get into the Happy-ever-after Home, perhaps an old lady could! Chuckling to himself, he hurried home to his den and rooted out the things he had stolen from Granny Riding Hood's cottage so long ago. He put on her nightgown and slippers, her curlers and her headscarf.

Then he grabbed her handbag and set off for the high road that led to the city.

He was waiting impatiently at the bus stop when up marched a squad of Girl Guides, led by a very large lady with a very red face.

'Troop, halt!' boomed the large lady. 'Now, pay attention, gels! A Girl Guide never misses the opportunity to do a good deed. For example, here we have an old woman too timid to cross the road by herself. Watch me closely.'

Marching up to the wolf she called out, 'Allow me to be of assistance, my good woman!'

'Eh?' said the wolf in surprise.

'Deaf as a post, gels,' announced the large lady, 'Though you wouldn't think it when you look at the size of her ears.'

'Who are you calling deaf?' growled the wolf crossly.

'Mad as a hatter too,' the large lady told her squad. 'Doesn't even know who she is!'

'Clear off!' growled the wolf.

'No need to be alarmed,' boomed the large lady. 'I am Group Captain Frobisher of the Girl Guides. You're quite safe with me. Just take my arm.'

The wolf looked at Group Captain Frobisher's large, beefy arm, and remembered that he hadn't had any breakfast.

'Coo, did you see that?' said a Girl Guide. 'That little old lady just swallowed Group Captain Frobisher!'

'Golly,' exclaimed another. 'She had jolly big teeth for such an old woman.'

'She didn't want to cross the road after all,' pointed out a third. 'Look, she's getting on a bus now!'

'I think,' said a fourth, who was wearing a red hood over her uniform, 'we'd better go and tell the woodcutter ... I mean, the police.'

Chapter Two

'Tickets, Please!'

Detective Chief Inspector Plonker was sitting in his office watching his favourite TV programme, *The Hex Files*, when his assistant, Detective Sergeant Snoop, poked his head around the door.

'Excuse me, sir,' said Sergeant Snoop.

'Yes, Sergeant, what is it?' snapped Inspector Plonker irritably, keeping one eye on the television.

'There's a Girl Guide in a red hood out here. She says an old lady ate her group captain at a bus stop,' said Sergeant Snoop.

'Don't be ridiculous, Snoop,' said Inspector Plonker. 'Old ladies don't eat Girl Guides at bus stops.'

'Perhaps she said "tuck shop",' said the sergeant, consulting his notebook.

'The point is, Snoop,' said Inspector Plonker, 'old ladies don't eat Girl Guides at all. Or boy scouts, for that matter. They eat teacakes, custard creams, that sort of thing.'

'But, sir,' said Sergeant Snoop, 'the Girl Guide says this wasn't a real old lady.'

'Well then, she couldn't have eaten anybody at a bus stop, could she?' said Inspector Plonker triumphantly.

'Well, er, I suppose not, sir,' replied Sergeant Snoop, scratching his head.

'Good man,' said Inspector Plonker. 'Now clear off. I'm busy.'

As Sergeant Snoop closed the door, Inspector Plonker turned his attention back to *The Hex Files*. This week's episode was the best yet. The hero, Special Agent Mildew, had watched his next-door neighbour sprouting hair, howling at the moon and eating the Avon Lady, and suspected that the man just might be a werewolf. Inspector Plonker wished he was as clever as that!

The wolf was sitting on the bus having a doze when somebody tapped him sharply on the shoulder and said, 'Tickets please.' The wolf opened his eyes and saw a small, fat, cranky little man in a shiny blue uniform and a peaked cap glaring at him.

'Tickets please, madam,' repeated the ticket inspector impatiently. 'Come along, we haven't got all day!'

The wolf rooted in Granny Riding Hood's handbag, found her bus pass, and handed it to the cranky little man.

The ticket inspector peered at it suspiciously. 'Hang on a minute, this doesn't look like you!' he said, looking from Granny's photo to the wolf and back again.

'Eh?' said the wolf.

'Your ears are too big, for a start,' the ticket inspector went on, 'and the lady in this picture doesn't have glowing red eyes.'

The wolf growled softly.

'That does it,' said the ticket inspector, placing his hand firmly on the wolf's shoulder. 'I can't tell from the photo whether this old lady is

Granny Riding Hood

growling or not, but she's definitely not foaming at the mouth. Driver, call the police!'

The wolf looked at the ticket inspector's pudgy fingers and remembered that he hadn't had any lunch.

'George,' said a woman in the back seat, nudging her husband, 'do you see that little old lady who's just getting off?'

'What about her?' asked George, without looking up from his newspaper.

'She just swallowed the ticket inspector,' said his wife.

'Good,' said George, turning to the sports page. 'Let's hope she goes and swallows a few traffic wardens while she's at it!'

'She has beautiful teeth for a woman of her age,' said his wife admiringly.

Chapter Three

PC Pimple

Sergeant Snoop opened the door just wide enough to poke his head through. 'Sorry to interrupt again, sir,' he said.

'What is it now, Snoop?' sighed Inspector Plonker. *The Hex Files* was getting more exciting by the minute. The werewolf, having devoured the vet, two zoo-keepers and an animal rights activist, was now being pursued by Agent Mildew through the moonlit city streets.

'A bus driver just radioed in to say that an old lady swallowed a ticket inspector on the number seventeen,' said Sergeant Snoop.

'I've told you before, Snoop,' said Inspector Plonker, 'old ladies don't eat –'

'Perhaps she doesn't *like* teacakes, sir,' interrupted Sergeant Snoop.

'Oh, very well then,' said Inspector Plonker. 'Send a few cars to investigate.'

'By the way, sir,' said Sergeant Snoop, 'that Girl Guide with the red hood is still outside and she says her granny –'

'Never mind that Girl Guide's granny,' snapped Inspector Plonker. 'Tell that Girl Guide to go and tie a granny knot in her granny. And don't interrupt me again.'

'No sir, I won't sir, yes sir,' said Sergeant Snoop.

The wolf was walking along the street towards the gates of the Happy-ever-after Home for Retired Fairy-tale Characters when he heard sirens wailing. A number of police cars screeched to a halt beside him. A young constable with pimples and a wispy moustache sprang out of the nearest car and blocked his path.

'Excuse me, madam,' he enquired, 'but did you just get off the number seventeen bus?'

'What's it to you?' answered the wolf crossly.

'*I'll* ask the questions, madam, *if* you don't mind!' barked the young constable in his best policeman voice. 'Now, is that a ticket inspector's cap you're chewing?'

The wolf gulped and swallowed something. 'Not chewing anything now,' he said sulkily.

'Aha, trying to be clever, eh?' said the young constable, grabbing hold of the wolf's collar. 'Well, maybe you'd better come down to the station with me and we'll see how clever you really are!'

The wolf looked at the constable's skinny wrist and realised that it was long past his dinner time.

Chapter Four

AAARGH!

Sergeant Snoop barged straight into Inspector Plonker's office, looking very agitated. 'I think you'd better come and listen to this right away, sir!' he said.

'Very well, Snoop,' said Inspector Plonker, turning off the television, '*The Hex Files* is over anyway.'

Agent Mildew had shot the werewolf with a silver bullet and saved the citizens of the city (except for those unfortunate enough to have been in the public library when the crowded school bus he was driving crashed into it and exploded during the Big Chase).

'Why can't we ever have any *exciting* crimes around here?' muttered the inspector as he followed Sergeant Snoop into the radio room. The Girl Guide with the red hood was sitting by the radio, listening intently.

'What's *she* doing here?' said Chief Inspector Plonker.

'Never mind her now, sir,' said Sergeant Snoop, picking up the microphone. 'Control to PC Briggs. What's the situation out there?'

'PC Briggs to Control,' gabbled an excited voice over the radio. 'An old lady just swallowed PC Pimple on the high street!'

Inspector Plonker snatched the microphone from the sergeant's hand.

'Plonker here!' he barked officiously. 'Now, pull yourself together, Briggs.

You say an old woman swallowed PC Pimple. You're sure it wasn't a teacake?'

'No, sir,' crackled the voice of PC Briggs. 'It was definitely an old woman, sir.'

'No, Briggs,' said the inspector, 'I mean, are you sure it was PC Pimple and not a ... Oh, never mind. What's happening now?'

'PC Bloggs is walking towards her, sir. He's taking out his notebook. He's ... she's just swallowed PC Bloggs, sir!'

'Calm down, Briggs,' said Inspector Plonker. 'Remember your training, man! Say "What's all this 'ere then?"'

'PC Purvis just did that, sir!'

'Well done, that man,' said the inspector. 'What happened?'

'She swallowed him, sir!'

'Right, Briggs,' said the inspector sternly, 'it's time to get tough. Tell her you're afraid you'll have to ask her to accompany you down to the station.'

'PC Wilks tried that one, sir!'

'And?'

'She swallowed him too, sir,' said Briggs, panic rising in his voice. 'She's coming this way, sir! She's swallowed PC Perkins, sir! She's right outside the car. She's swallowed PC AAARGH!'

The radio spluttered, crackled and died. Inspector Plonker looked puzzled. 'Don't remember him,' he said.

'Who, sir?' asked Sergeant Snoop, staring in horror at the silent radio.

'PC AAARGH!' said the inspector. 'Must be a new recruit.'

Chapter Five

Full Moon

'Excuse me, Inspector,' said the Girl Guide with the red hood, who had been listening the whole time, 'I think I know what's going on here. You see, my granny used to live in the forest, and there was this wolf …'

But Inspector Plonker wasn't listening. He was staring out the window, where night had fallen and a full moon was shining brightly over the city. Suddenly he whirled around and smacked his fist into his palm.

'Snoop,' he cried, 'I am a complete idiot!'

'Yes sir.'

'What d'you mean, "Yes sir," Snoop?'

'Sorry, sir, I mean, no sir, sir,' smirked Sergeant Snoop.

'Don't you see?' said the inspector excitedly, 'it's just like that episode of *The Hex Files* I've been watching!'

'Beg pardon, sir,' said Sergeant Snoop carefully, 'but do you really think you should base any more investigations on episodes of *The Hex Files*? I mean, look what happened last time.'

'What are you driving at, Snoop?' demanded Inspector Plonker crossly.

'Well, sir,' said the sergeant, 'there was that fellow you charged with being a fiendish, blood-sucking, grave-robbing zombie in a built-up area ...'

'I remember him,' said Inspector Plonker. 'Shifty-looking character. Always hanging around cemeteries with a shovel.'

'He was a grave-digger, sir.'

'Yes, well, we all make mistakes, Snoop.'

'Yes sir,' continued Sergeant Snoop, 'but do you remember that bloke you arrested for being the flesh-eating mummy of King Tut in a manner likely to lead to a breach of the peace, sir?'

'Never forget him,' replied the inspector, 'lurching along the street, wrapped from head to toe in filthy bandages, moaning to himself.'

'He'd fallen out of the back of an ambulance while being rushed to hospital after a steamroller ran over him, sir!'

'Well,' said the inspector reasonably, 'at least I didn't actually drive that stake through his heart.'

'Only because I wouldn't hold it steady for you, sir.'

'Anyway, never mind all that now, Snoop,' said Inspector Plonker. 'This time I *know* what we're up against.'

'I suppose you mean a wolfman, sir?' said Sergeant Snoop wearily.

'No, Snoop,' said the inspector. 'I mean something even more vicious, more bestial, more mindlessly savage!'

'Football supporters, sir?'

'No, Snoop,' said Inspector Plonker, 'I mean ... the Wolfgran!'

'Idiot!' muttered the Girl Guide with the red hood, as she slipped unnoticed out the door and hurried off into the night.

Chapter Six

'Wolf! Wolf!'

The wolf bounded up the steps of the Happy-ever-after Home for Retired Fairy-tale Characters. He pushed his way through the revolving doors into the lobby. Visiting time was over, and the corridors were deserted as he prowled around, searching for Granny Riding Hood's room.

Suddenly, a voice boomed: 'Granny Riding Hood, where do we think we are going?'

A large, beefy matron with a red face, who looked exactly like Group Captain

Frobisher (and was, in fact, her twin sister), came striding up to the wolf, clutching a medicine bottle and a spoon. 'Sneaking out to the loo again, were we?' she scolded, wagging her finger. 'Naughty, naughty! We must learn to use our bedpan after lights out, mustn't we?'

'Eh?' said the wolf.

'We *were* going to have our medicine in our nice, cosy bed,' continued the matron. 'But, as we've been so naughty, we'll just have to take it out here in the nasty, cold corridor, won't we?'

'Don't want any!' growled the wolf sulkily.

'Now, now,' said the matron, pouring medicine onto the spoon and holding it out to the wolf, 'let's do what matron says, hmm? Open wide and swallow.'

The wolf shrugged and did what he was told. After all, it was nearly suppertime.

Nurse Cotton, the night nurse, was sitting at her desk, reading a paperback about a nurse who falls in love with a tall, dark, handsome brain surgeon – and wondering why all *she* ever met were small, fat, balding bowel-specialists – when she saw the little old man hobbling down the corridor towards her.

'Wolf! Wolf!' cried the little old man hoarsely. 'A wolf just swallowed matron, over by the women's ward!'

'Yes dear, I know all about it,' said Nurse Cotton soothingly. 'Just cut

along back to bed now, and I'll be along in a minute to tuck you in.'

Nurse Cotton shook her head sadly as she watched him scuttling obediently away. The Old Boy Who Cried Wolf had been playing that same trick ever since he was a lad. Didn't he realise that nobody believed him any more?

The wolf opened the door and crept quietly into Granny Riding Hood's room.

'Hello, Granny,' he growled.

'Eh? What? Who's there?' exclaimed Granny, waking with a start.

'It is I, Little Red Riding Hood,' said the wolf in his squeakiest voice, which sounded like a duck being throttled.

'Oh, it's you, granddaughter,' said Granny. 'I didn't recognise you. I'm blind as a bat without me glasses.'

'I've brought you something nice to eat, Granny,' squeaked the wolf huskily.

'Eh, what's that?' said Granny. 'You'll have to speak up, dear. I'm deaf as a post without me hearing aid.'

'Would you like some toffee, Granny?' squeaked the wolf, creeping towards the bed.

'Toffee?' replied Granny. 'Don't be silly, girl! You know it gets stuck in me dentures.'

The wolf grinned and leaned over the bed.

'Gracious, girl!' said Granny, 'your breath smells of bus conductors! But you've certainly got a grand set of teeth!'

'All the better to eat you with,' growled the wolf.

'Oh no!' said Granny Riding Hood. 'Not *you* again!'

Chapter Seven

Silver Bullets

'Begging your pardon, sir,' said Sergeant Snoop. 'We've carried out your orders.'

'Good man, Snoop,' said Inspector Plonker, who was peering down the barrel of a large, black revolver. 'Every old lady in the city locked up in the cells, eh?'

'Yes, sir,' said Sergeant Snoop, looking nervously at the gun. 'They were none too pleased about it either. Most of 'em were on their way to bingo.'

'Never mind bingo, Snoop,' said the inspector. 'The safety of the city is more important than bingo! One of those old ladies is the Wolfgran, and I'm going to keep 'em all here 'till I find out which one.'

'Yes, sir,' said Sergeant Snoop, standing to attention and clicking his heels together.

'By the way,' continued Inspector Plonker, 'did you get any of 'em to talk yet?'

Sergeant Snoop looked embarrassed. 'Only about their waterworks, sir.'

'Their what?' exclaimed the inspector.

'You know, sir,' said Sergeant Snoop, blushing bright red, 'their *plumbing*.'

'What do they think we are, Snoop, sanitary inspectors?'

'Operations, sir,' stammered Sergeant Snoop. 'You know, tubes in their ...'

'Yes, yes, that will do, Snoop,' said the inspector hastily. 'By the way, you know that silver trophy in the canteen?'

'The trophy I won in the station ping-pong tournament, sir?'

'That's the one,' said the inspector. 'Have it melted down immediately. I'll need some silver bullets for this gun.'

'Yes, sir,' said Sergeant Snoop, gloomily.

'Don't sulk, Snoop,' said the inspector sternly. 'The safety of the city is more important than ping-pong!'

'Yes, sir.'

'Oh, and Snoop?'

'Sir?'

'The minute one of 'em swallows you, come and let me know!'

Chapter Eight

Bedpanned!

The Girl Guide in the red hood crept into Granny Riding Hood's room in the Happy-ever-after Home. She peered suspiciously at the figure snoring loudly in the bed. It certainly looked like her grandmother (for, of course, the Girl Guide was none other than Little Red Riding Hood). At any rate the creature was wearing her granny's nightcap and nightdress, but she thought she'd better make sure.

'Grandmother?' she whispered softly.

The wolf (who had been sleeping off a bout of indigestion) woke at once and opened his glowing red eyes. 'Why, granddaughter,' he said in a shrill, quavery voice, 'how lovely to see you. Come over and give me a kiss. I hope you've brought me some toffee!'

'Oh, Granny,' said Little Red Riding Hood, 'I'm so glad you're safe. The wolf is in the city, hunting for you. I tried to tell the police, but they just wouldn't listen!'

'Never mind that now, dearie,' quavered the wolf. 'You just come over here and give your old granny a hug.'

Little Red Riding Hood moved towards the bed.

The wolf reached out for her. He narrowed his eyes, bared his teeth and was just starting to drool when Little Red Riding Hood hit him over the head with the bedpan.

'But how did you know?' asked a shocked Nurse Cotton, who had come rushing down the corridor to Granny's room when Little Red Riding Hood pressed the buzzer. 'It's such a marvellous disguise! In fact, the only person who saw through it was The Old Boy Who Cried Wolf.'

Little Red Riding Hood looked over at the wolf, who was lying unconscious in the bed. 'It was quite simple really,' she replied. 'My Granny is blind as a bat without her spectacles, deaf as a post without her hearing aid, and can't eat toffee because of her false teeth. As you can see, her hearing aid and spectacles are still on the bedside table. Yet, the wolf heard me when I whispered, recognised me as soon as he opened his eyes – even though I was standing by the door – and the first thing he asked me for was toffee.'

'Brilliant!' said Nurse Cotton admiringly.

'Besides,' continued Little Red Riding Hood, 'I know for a fact that Granny doesn't have one of those!' And she pointed to the end of the bed where, sticking out from underneath the covers, was the wolf's long, shaggy tail!

'But what has happened to your granny?' asked Nurse Cotton.

'Oh, he's swallowed her, I expect,' said Little Red Riding Hood cheerfully.

'Oh my, how awful!' exclaimed the nurse.

'He's swallowed your matron too, I should think,' Little Red Riding Hood went on, 'and he swallowed Group Captain Frobisher, a ticket inspector, and ever so many policemen!'

'But what can we do?' wailed Nurse Cotton in despair.

'You forget that he's a fairy-tale wolf,' said Little Red Riding Hood. 'They're all quite safe. All you have to do is cut him open and out they'll pop.'

'Cut him open?' Nurse Cotton shrieked in horror.

'Don't worry,' grinned Little Red Riding Hood, 'he's used to it. Have you got a scissors?'

Chapter Nine

'Freeze!'

'Excuse me, sir,' said Sergeant Snoop.

'What is it now, Snoop?' said Chief Inspector Plonker, who was busily loading his revolver with silver bullets. 'They can't all want to go *again*. They've only just been.'

'It's not that, sir,' said Sergeant Snoop, looking at the bullets and thinking sadly of his ping-pong trophy. 'PC Pimple's on the radio.'

'PC Pimple?' exclaimed the inspector. 'I thought he'd been swallowed!'

'It seems he's been regurgitated, sir.'

'Can't say I'm surprised,' said Inspector Plonker. 'I could never stomach the fellow myself. What does he want?'

'He says they've captured the Wolfgran, sir,' said sergeant Snoop. 'She's at the Happy-ever-after Home, apparently.'

'Right,' said the inspector, leaping to his feet and shoving the loaded revolver into his pocket. 'Come on, Snoop, duty calls!'

'I'm not staying in this place another minute,' said Granny Riding Hood, hurrying down the steps of the Happy-ever-after Home, hand-in-hand with her granddaughter. 'I'll be safer in me cottage. And at least I won't have that matron trying to poison me with medicine every night.'

'Freeze!' yelled Inspector Plonker, leaping out of the darkness brandishing his revolver. 'Not you, you idiots!' he added, as PCs Pimple, Bloggs, Purvis, Wilks, Perkins and Briggs (who had been on their way back to the station for a refreshing cup of tea) all sprang to attention with their hands up.

'What's that man saying, dear?' said Granny to Little Red Riding Hood.

'I think he wants you to freeze, Grandma,' Little Red Riding Hood replied.

'Oh, he does, does he?' said Granny. 'Well, he needn't think I'm taking off me nice warm coat in *this* weather!'

'Silence, you fiendish ... er ... fiend!' screamed Inspector Plonker. 'Another word out of you and I'll drill you full of lead ... er ... I mean, silver!'

'How dare you speak to this nice old lady like that!' cried Group Captain Frobisher, who had just come through the door with Matron and the ticket inspector. 'It's easy to see you were never a Girl Guide.'

'This nice old lady, as you call her, is a werewolf,' said Inspector Plonker. 'Now stand back while I blast her!'

'You will do no such thing,' said Matron sternly. 'This lady is a resident of mine and I will not have my residents massacred on the premises by deranged policemen. It gives the home a bad name.'

'You're telling me this isn't the Wolfgran?' said Inspector Plonker.

'The creature to whom you refer,' replied Matron coldly, 'is at present in the room at the end of the corridor. He is recovering from a serious operation performed by this remarkable little girl.'

'Good show, Riding Hood,' said Group Captain Frobisher. 'I'll see you get your first-aid badge for this.'

'He tried to use a stolen bus pass, you know,' said the ticket inspector. 'That's a criminal offence, that is!'

'Right,' said Inspector Plonker. 'Follow me, Snoop!'

He rushed down the corridor, with Sergeant Snoop and Little Red Riding Hood hard on his heels, and burst into Granny Riding Hood's room. But the rumpled bed was empty, and the curtains were flapping in a breeze that blew through the open window.

'Escaped!' said Chief Inspector Plonker. 'This kind of thing never happens on *The Hex Files*.'

'He must have sneaked out the window while we were outside,' said Little Red Riding Hood. 'He'll be back in the forest by now.'

'Nonsense,' said Inspector Plonker grimly. 'As far as I'm concerned, the Wolfgran is still at large in this city, and I will hunt her down if it takes the rest of my life! Right, Snoop?'

'Yes, sir,' said Sergeant Snoop, rolling his eyes up to heaven.

Chapter Ten

Scary Old Ladies

Thanks to Chief Inspector Plonker, who held a press conference on the steps of the Happy-ever-after Home that very night, the people of the city were soon convinced that a werewolf, disguised as a harmless old lady, was on the loose in their midst.

As a result, old ladies found that people were a lot more willing to give up their seats to them on buses, and nobody ever objected when they skipped the queue in supermarkets, or spent half an hour counting their pensions at crowded post-office counters. Of course, people also stopped helping them across busy roads. But, since every car, bus, bicycle and lorry immediately screeched to a halt, or sped off in the opposite direction, if an old lady so much as appeared on the pavement, they found they didn't need that kind of help any more.

As for Granny Riding Hood, she returned to the forest and managed to buy her cottage back from the Three Little Pigs. The wolf had decided that dressing up as a little old lady was far too dangerous, so she didn't have to worry about him any more. However, as the Three Little Pigs had small brains and short memories, they immediately spent all their money on straw, used it to build an enormous block of flats and invited all their relatives to come and live with them.

So, in the end, the wolf was never short of something to eat, and he soon found that pork was much easier on the digestion than policemen.

THE END

The Wolfgran:
Who's Who

Granny Riding Hood

Granny Riding Hood, as we all know, lived happily in her little cottage in the forest until the day the wolf showed up on her doorstep, pretending to be her granddaughter. Nobody is really sure what happened after that. Granny always said that the wolf was so hungry he swallowed her whole, without even chewing. But, as she also said his stomach was full of old clothes and mothballs, it's possible that he just stuffed her into the wardrobe instead. (Old ladies often get confused about that kind of thing!)

Little Red Riding Hood

What we do know for sure is that, once he had disposed of Granny, the wolf put on her nightie and hopped into her bed to wait for Little Red Riding Hood, who arrived soon afterwards. It must have been pretty dark in that cottage because, at first, Little Red Riding Hood actually thought that the huge hairy beast growling at her from the bed really was her grandmother. In fact she didn't start getting suspicious until the wolf tried to eat her, and even then she thought it was only Granny having one of her funny turns. Luckily a passing woodcutter, who saw her desperately trying to persuade the slavering wolf to go back to bed and finish his Ovaltine, came rushing to the rescue.

The Wolf

Now, have you ever wondered how anybody could mistake a wolf for their granny, granddaughter or indeed any other member of the family? Of course, as we've already said, old ladies sometimes get confused, but even Granny must have known the difference between a little girl and a big, ferocious animal. As for Little Red Riding Hood, if you were out walking all alone along a dark forest path and a wolf came slinking out of the shadows and asked where you were going, would you tell him? I didn't think so! So why weren't Granny and Little Red Riding Hood more cautious when it came to wolves?

The Old Boy Who Cried Wolf

Well, it was all the fault of The Old Boy Who Cried Wolf. He was a practical joker, who only knew one joke. He spent all his time trying to convince people that there was a wolf about. When he wasn't yelling 'Wolf! Wolf! Run for your lives!' and then laughing his head off as everybody started climbing trees and hiding under beds, he was howling like a wolf outside people's windows and growling like a wolf outside their doors. In the end, everybody got so sick of him and his tricks that they gave up believing there were any real wolves in the forest at all. This meant that when the wolf actually did come calling, people just laughed and said things like, 'Oh yeah, very funny! You don't think I'm going to fall for that one again, do you?' Sometimes they even said, 'Take that silly mask off, for goodness' sake!' and started pulling his ears! The wolf found this a bit odd, but, as it made his dinners much easier to come by, he wasn't complaining!

The Three Little Pigs

In fact, the only people in the forest who seemed to take the wolf at all seriously were the Three Little Pigs. The Three Little Pigs were building contractors and, whenever one of the houses they built was blown down by the wind (which seemed to happen pretty often), they always blamed the wolf. 'That old rogue,' they would say, shaking their heads as they looked at the ruins, 'He's been out huffing and puffing again!' When a customer suggested that maybe the houses blew down because they were only built of sticks and straw, the three pigs would take out their calculators and say, 'Oh, you wanted a wolf-proof house did you? You should have said. Well, now, that'll cost extra, you know!' They would then charge the poor customer twice as much as before for the proper house of bricks that they should have built in the first place!

So it seems that the wolf is the cause of all the trouble in the forest, mainly because he is always trying to eat somebody! But he has a pretty hard time trying to get a decent meal. He may well have swallowed Granny, but he certainly didn't have time to digest her (Ugh!). He never got his paws on Little Red Riding Hood or the Three Little Pigs and, if you believe the stories, some really horrible things happened to him while he was after them. (I don't want to go into all that here, but just imagine how you'd feel if somebody sewed a lot of rocks into your stomach and dropped you down a well! Or how would you like falling down a chimney into a cauldron of boiling soup?) Despite everything, it seems that the old villain is still on the prowl and, let's face it, by now he must be pretty cross and very, very hungry indeed!